GRANDFATHER'S TROLLEY

Written and photo-illustrated by Bruce McMillan

CANDLEWICK PRESS
CAMBRIDGE, MASSACHUSETTS

I remember . . .

When I was a little girl, I used to
visit my grandfather at work.
I waited and listened
for the trolley.

Toot! Toot!

The trolley car rolled around
the bend. Grandfather was
the motorman.
"Hi, darlin'. Your seat's waitin'
for you. Hop aboard!"

I liked to sit way in back.
Grandfather always saved
a seat in the last row
— over the 8 —
just for me.

Ding ding!
Gong gong!

The trolley bells rang,
and we started
to move.

I held on tight. I pretended
that I was motoring the trolley
car, just like Grandfather.

**Clackety-clackety,
clackety-clack.**

The woods sped by.

I leaned back and
squinted to keep the
breeze out of my eyes.
The trolley car swayed
from side to side.

**_Clackety-clackety,
clackety-clack._**

I rocked with the car
from side to side.

**_Clackety-clackety,
clackety-clack._**

At the end of the line,
Grandfather helped me down.
"Watch your step, darlin'.
Don't go too near the water."
Soon I heard him call, "All ready
for my number one helper!"

I brought the power
controls from one end
of the car to the other,
where Grandfather
was waiting.
"Thank you, number one."

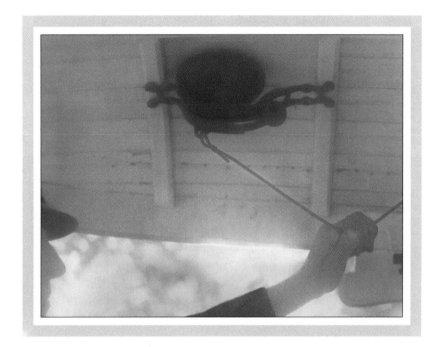

The conductor
adjusted the trolley poles,
and the trolley car faced
back the way we'd come.
It was ready to go.

Ding ∂ing! Gong gong!

On the ride back I sat up front
next to Grandfather.

Clackety-clackety, clackety-clack.

The wind blew hard.
Grandfather called back to me,
"I hope your hair ribbon's on tight!"

At the stop before mine,
Grandfather made room
for me by the controls.
Together, we motored
the trolley car.
Grandfather called out,
"Full speed ahead!"

***Clackety-clackety,
clackety-clack!***

The breeze blew by.
We sped along.
And then I saw my stop.

Grandfather
jumped off and
held out his arms.
"Free ride down for my
number one helper."
His whiskers tickled
when I hugged him.
I said, "Thank you,
Grandfather."

Before he started
the trolley again,
Grandfather watched
me run home down
the lane. I never had
to look back to see if
he was watching me.
I just knew. . . .

He was my grandfather.

A Note from the Author

The trolley car in this book, Connecticut Trolley 838, was built in 1905 by J. M. Jones Sons, West Troy, New York. Its last Connecticut runs transported football fans to and from the Yale Bowl in 1946. In 1975 the car was fully restored by the Seashore Trolley Museum, located near Kennebunkport, Maine. It remains there today, and because this is a working museum, visitors may still ride on trolley car 838.